KNUCKLEHEAD DAD and the Adventures of SHARKMAID!

By Tommy Forys

Knucklehead Dad and the Adventures of Sharkmaid!

ISBN: 9781793958655
Text & Illustration © 2019 by Thomas J. Forys Jr.
Editing by his Mommy, Janeen.

This book is dedicated to my wife, Jackie, and my wee ones, Olivia & Logan.
Thanks for allowing me the time and space to give it a go.

It's perfectly OK to be a knucklehead sometimes, and make friends laugh.

Knucklehead
APPROVED!

"Our dad constantly tries to make us laugh by being goofy. He could be dancing, inventing songs with crazy words or even drawing silly pictures. He's really, REALLY good at being a Knucklehead Dad".

– The Kids

As the family awaits their order at the restaurant, the kids again pester Knucklehead Dad to draw their favorite things with crayons. Climbing on him and pleading in opposing ears, he hears "Dad, draw a great white shark!", "NO Daddy, draw a mermaid PLEEEEASSSE?" Mommy expertly tunes out the madness and orders some more to drink. She sure does like grape juice!

Aggravated, but feeling silly and a little lazy, Knucklehead Dad combines both kids' request into one crazy creature combination. Dad invents on-the-fly a character he calls "Sharkmaid". He begins to draw the half mermaid, half shark creature as his kids look excitedly over his shoulder. What adventures await Sharkmaid, only Daddy knows. As the kids watch, the fun begins...

Human kids like to play at the park. Many more like to eat ice cream, go to the movies and play games with friends. Sharks like to have fun too. Fun for some sharks means messing with Captain Squint, the "shark expert" who works for the aquarium. Squint tries to capture sharks for exhibits, but they usually just swim away and laugh. Today, Squint has a special visitor.

Bored dodging Squint's net, sharks swim away in search of a snack. To Squint's surprise, one fascinating critter stays behind. Out of the water pops a half shark, half mermaid. "WHOA!", Squint screams. "I've seen dogfish, catfish, sea lions, parrot fish, and sea cows, but I have never seen a Sharkmaid!". Squint and Sharkmaid eagerly bump knuckles.

Sharkmaid tells how that very morning he woke mysteriously in a bed of seaweed to discover he's somehow changed. "I'm a little freaked out" he admits. Sympathetic, Squint suggests a visit to Mermaid City deep below. "King Neptune has magical powers and can probably help". Sharkmaid was jazzed. "But remember, mermaids REALLY hate sharks" informs Squint.

As Sharkmaid descends into the ocean, he reminds himself to blend in with the REAL mermaids in order to have a chance to meet King Neptune. Finding a bunch of rhodophyta (red algae) on the ocean floor, he ties together a wig that resembles gorgeous, flowing red mermaid hair...sort of. An onlooking octopus, sea horse and exotic fish are thoroughly confused.

"I'm wigged out and feeling goofy, wonder what's next," he asks himself. Everybody knows that mermaids wear shellkinis as part of their swimming attire. Accepting this, Sharkmaid does his best to fashion a shellkini of his own using seaweed and some oddly shaped shells found on the ocean floor. A nearby dolphin, sea turtle and eel simply cannot believe their eyes.

Taking a deep breath of water for courage, Sharkmaid swims into the Mermaid City. He's momentarily distracted by the delicious smells coming from the kitchen. Mermaids are known for making magnificent, marvelous, and magical baked goods. They stay warm and dry even in the coldest and deepest waters. The yummy aroma bubbles float around for all to sniff.

Swimming into the main ballroom, Sharkmaid gets more than a few strange looks from the mermaids. Even with his wacky wig and silly shellkini, the mermaids welcome him as one their own with perfect, pearly-white smiles. Soon, oodles of pies, brownies, cookies, and cakes arrive. Sharkmaid does his best not to gorge on the treats and resist his very shark-like instincts.

Sharkmaid is proud of his composure even as many tempting smells dance around his nose. Complete success...that is until somebody announces the arrival of fresh, hot, flavorful, magic donuts! Sharkmaid's eyes spin as he completely loses his mind. A chorus of "DOOOO-nut, DOOOO-nut, donut, donut, donut, donut, DOOOO-NUT, donut, donut, donut" plays in his head.

No longer able to control himself, Sharkmaid leaps onto the sweets table and grabs a handful of donuts even before the crowd has a chance to smell them. Soon he is gobbling platefuls of those sweet confections while the mermaids look at him with utter disgust. Ashamed, all he could think to say was "What? I tripped!" With red cheeks and a full belly, he swims away.

Leaving the embarrassing situation behind, Sharkmaid wanders into a game room where mermaids are playing cards. A friendly group invites him to play a few hands and boy, does he ever! Winning game after game, he boasts loudly to all of Mermaid City "I am the undisputed poker champion, y'all!" An irked mermaid mutters "card shark" under her breath.

Thirsty from victory, Sharkmaid searches for some soda pop. He stumbles upon a sorrowful mermaid holding her injured tail. "Bad move fencing with a sword fish" she said. Most sharks smelling a boo-boo would take a bite, but Sharkmaid just wants to help. "Are you a nurse?", she asks. "I'm no nurse, I'm a great whi, whi, errr whiii-stler" he said, horribly whistling a tune.

Finally, Sharkmaid finds a Zip-Zap Soda machine. A pink-haired mermaid wants a soda too, but she seems annoyed. "I don't have any coins, can you lend me one?", she asks. "Tell you what, I'll give you a gold doubloon but you have to pay me back 6,289 donuts by tomorrow night," he replies. More irritated now than ever, she screams "loan shark", and leaves thirsty.

Though only half shark, Sharkmaid still exhibits many common shark traits. In a great white shark's lifetime, one might grow as many as 20,000 individual teeth! Two puzzled mermaids discover a freshly discarded shark's tooth lying on the ocean floor near the ballroom. "What on Earth is this doing here?" she asks. "No clue," says a smiling Sharkmaid.

Hurrying excitedly into the courtyard, Sharkmaid overhears that King Neptune is about to give his speech. This might be his only chance to ask the mermaid king for help turning back into a shark. As Neptune passes by, his trident accidentally catches Sharkmaid's rhodophyta wig and pulls it off. Everybody stares in horror as Sharkmaid's true identity is revealed.

Sharkmaid does his best to explain himself to the crowd of irate mermaids, but as their shouting grows louder, he has no chance to be heard. Instead, King Neptune points his trident directly at Sharkmaid and orders him to leave Mermaid City immediately and never return. Sad and dejected, Sharkmaid looks upon the furious, red-faced mermaids and agrees to leave.

Now far, far away, a teary-eyed Sharkmaid looks back one last time. To his surprise, he sees a huge army of jellyfish descending upon Mermaid City. "Those jellies are crashing the party!" he growls. Sharkmaid now has a tough decision to make. Keep swimming away as ordered or turn back and help fight those nasty, jiggly, party-crashing jellies. What would you do?

Sharkmaid decides that helping is the right thing to do, even if he was treated very poorly. Besides all that, he's hungry. On his way back, he can't help but make a pit stop in the kitchen. Sharkmaid enjoys a few more donuts (just because), and also grabs a jar of peanut butter. Why peanut butter you ask? Well, you tell me what goes better with jellies?

Bursting loudly through the kitchen doors and out into the jelly-infested city, Sharkmaid screams "GET INTO MY BELLY, JELLIES!" He ties a napkin around his neck as he takes a long look at the jellyfish as each tries to land on the mermaid's heads. He cries through gritted teeth "NOW!" and kicks into action with a determined wave of his mermaid tail.

Sharkmaid swims smoothly and swiftly as he grabs, bites and swallows jellyfish with every snap of his jaws. He even plucks surrounding jellies with his mermaid tail. "This tail isn't so bad after all," he mutters to himself. Making a squishy face after eating a sour jellyfish, he declares "those over-ripened ones will go down best with a creamy dollop of peanut butter."

Nobody believes their eyes, especially the lobster, pufferfish and marlin lurking nearby. Jellyfish disappear into Sharkmaid's belly like stars vanishing with every sunrise. Always concerned about dental health, Sharkmaid takes time to floss after his meal. "Ugh, absolutely nothing worse than jellyfish tentacles between your teeth!" he laughs to himself.

When the chaos settles down, grateful mermaids from all directions gather around their hero. Some mermaids lift Sharkmaid up and float him directly in front of King Neptune, who celebrates the victory. Sharkmaid uses this opportunity to explain his dilemma and ask for Neptune's help in making him a great white shark once more. "I can help you, dude," says Neptune.

The humbled king first asks "would you consider staying as my personal body guard?" "All-you-can-eat donuts is my only requirement," counters Sharkmaid. "You'll bankrupt us in a week, big guy," quips Neptune. The King winks as he aims his trident at Sharkmaid's belly. With a nod from Sharkmaid, a burst of brilliant yellow light blasts from the magic trident.

The energy erupting from Neptune's trident is so powerful, it hurls Sharkmaid through the ocean and into the blue skies above. A pelican and duck flying by are nearly knocked out of the air as Sharkmaid glides into their flight path. Wait a minute, is that a penguin I see? I thought penguins couldn't fly! Ones that surf on Sharkmaid's ginormous head can!

Tumbling back to Earth and settling deep onto the ocean bottom, Sharkmaid just feels different. Certainly a little more yellow, glowing and tingly than before, he exclaims "I feel like I have a thousand electric eels ferociously biting me, but in a good way." The stingray who saw it all says "that guy changed from SOMETHING into a shark right before my very eyes!"

"I'm BACK, bay-bay" thinks Sharkmaid, as the yellow glow that once consumed his entire body gradually fades away completely. King Neptune's magic actually worked! Fully transformed and free, the great white shark formerly known as Sharkmaid heads into the deep blue sea with a new sense of purpose and renewed eagerness for life. That and he just likes swimming

With no responsibilities beyond eating, swimming, raising baby sharks and terrorizing innocent beachgoers, this great white shark is again in his happy place...or is he? Do you think regular sharks seek fun adventures and laughs with friends? Do regular sharks like to play cards, drink soda or dine on delicious donuts? Uh, no. I wonder if we'll see Sharkmaid again.

Made in the USA
Lexington, KY
31 August 2019